W9-AID-810

123
versus
ABC

For my wife, Natalie, who is #1 and A+ in my book

 For information address HarperCollins Children's Books, a division of HarperCollins Publishers, 10 East 53rd Street, New York, NY 10022. www.harpercollinschildrens.com
Library of Congress Cataloging-in-Publication Data is available. ISBN 978-0-06-210299-7
The artist used Corel Painter to digitally create the illustrations for this book.
Typography by Dana Fritts. 13 14 15 16 17 SCP 10 9 8 7 6 5 4 3 2 1 ❖ First Edition

Mike Boldt

A versus B C

Hi! I'm so happy you chose to read this book about Letters.

HARPER
An Imprint of HarperCollinsPublishers

WHAT?!!

No no, there must be a mistake here. This book is about magnificent **Numbers!** We count and measure and add and subtract!

The mistake is all yours. This book is about lovely **Letters!** We make up the alphabet so you can spell and read!

About *Letters?* Why would all of us Numbers be here if this was about *Letters?*

Numbers in a book. That's laughable. As you can see, we Letters are here as well. In fact, today is Bring Your Lowercase to Work Day. Here's little a.

Numbers!

Letters!

Numbers numbers

NUMBERS!

Letters letters

LETTERS!

Umm . . . hello?

I'm not sure. I'm just the one Alligator who was asked to be in this book.

That settles it then. Since there is 1 Alligator, this is a book about Numbers.

Did you hear what you said?
Alligator. That starts
with the letter **A.** Just look
who else is showing up now.

Bears. B!
2 of them. They arrived in those 3 Cars.
Cars. Which Letter does the word Car start with again? Oh yeah. C.

ICE CREAM!

Now look! This is getting better for us Letters. After C comes D and E, right? Those would be Dinosaurs carrying—

4 Dinosaurs carrying
5 Eggs. Followed by
6 toads . . . and . . .

You mean
FROGS!

. . . 7 hungry Geese eating those 8 Hot dogs and
9 Ice-cream cones.

a, b, c, d, e, f, G(Geese)! H(Hot dog)! I(Ice cream)! And what's that? A Jigsaw puzzle being put together by Koalas and Lions.

A 10-piece Jigsaw puzzle being put together by 11 Koalas and 12 Lions. Why don't you just quit? Then you won't have to count those 13

Monkeys

wearing 14

Neckties

and juggling 15

Oranges

and the 16 Pigs
and the 17 Queens

18
Robots wearing Sombreros
19 sombreros actually,

20
Turtles

21 Unicycles with
22 Violins being played by
23 Wolves who are also playing all
24 of those Xylophones!

This is getting ridiculous.
I agree. Why would anyone need 25 balls of Yarn?
To knit sweaters for those 26 . . .

Zebras!!!

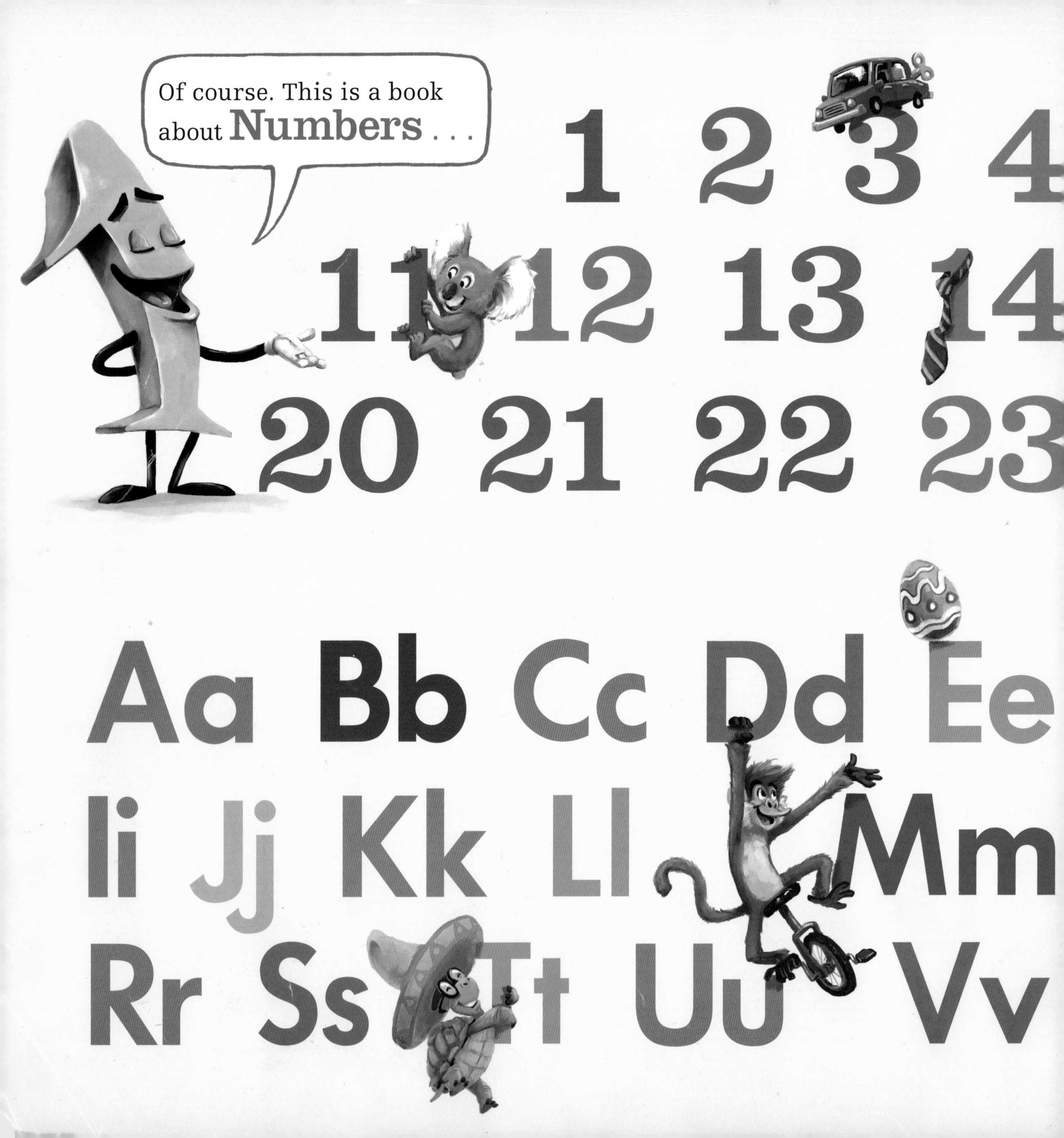
Of course. This is a book about Numbers . . .
1 2 3 4
11 12 13 14
20 21 22 23
Aa Bb Cc Dd Ee
Ii Jj Kk Ll Mm
Rr Ss Tt Uu Vv

5 6 7 8 9 10
15 16 17 18 19
24 25 26
. . . and Letters!
Ff Gg Hh
Nn Oo Pp Qq
Ww Xx Yy Zz

Well, it's sorted now at least.
What do you say we call it a day?

Umm . . . hello?
I'm a little lost. I'm
supposed to be in a
book about colors.